our
generation®

This is Ashley-Rose's story.

D1712100

ASHLEY-ROSE™

THE JUKEBOX BABYSITTERS

BY

SUSAN CAPPADONIA LOVE

ILLUSTRATED BY TRISH ROUELLE

An Our Generation® *book*

BATTAT INCORPORATED *Publisher*

A very special thanks to the editor,
Joanne Burke Casey.

Our Generation® Books is a registered trademark of Battat Incorporated.
Text copyright © 2011 by Susan Love
ISBN: 978-0-9844904-2-4
Printed in China

To sweet Juliette

Read all the adventures in the
Our Generation® Book Series

CONTENTS

EXTRA! EXTRA! READ ALL ABOUT IT!
Big words, wacky words, powerful words, funny words...
what do they all mean? They are marked with this symbol *.
Look them up in the Glossary at the end of this book.

Chapter One

FRIDAY AFTERNOON FLUB*

Even before I shoved my hand into the pocket of my jeans, I was 100% certain that I wouldn't feel the key in there.

How could I be so sure? Because from where I stood on the top step at Mr. and Mrs. Dott's back door, I could see the house key through their window.

It was on the kitchen table, right where I'd left it before I'd rushed through the room, slammed the back door and locked my cousin Katie, the four kids I was helping her babysit, their dog Jingles, and myself, out of the house.

"Ashley-Rose!" Katie yelped to me. "Please open the door! Quickly!"

I closed my eyes, took a deep breath, and tried to turn the doorknob. Hoping. Wishing. But of course a locked door cannot be opened without its key. I'd flubbed up. Again.

I was about to explain the problem to Katie, but she had already turned her attention back to a heated* argument.

The five-and-a-half-year-old twin brothers in our care were wrestling. Jack had Patrick pinned on the ground. He was trying to pry a yellow racecar out of Patrick's small fist.

"Jack," Katie said in a soothing voice, "*your* racecar is in the house. Let's go inside and get it."

Katie is a member of the Nickel Street Babysitters, the babysitting club in our neighborhood. It's called the NSB and includes Katie's five friends who also live here on Nickel Street.

They run a Junior Babysitters club for the younger girls, which I'm part of, and we get to help at babysitting jobs as long as we follow the rules: 1) all of our homework is done and 2) we are back home by 7:30 p.m. so we aren't out too late.

Someday I will be an official NSB member and babysit kids on my own. I can't wait! But as I looked on helplessly at the situation in the Dotts' yard, I thought, *Someday seems like a million years away!*

Dark clouds had begun dumping bucketsful of rain. Wind was blowing a flurry* of pink blossoms off the trees. Jingles was shaking water from his coat and it was spraying all over Violet, the baby.

Violet was crying at the top of her lungs. Her chubby cheeks were beet-red. She was kicking her feet wildly in the stroller. Violet wanted a bottle and she wanted it RIGHT AWAY!

Her three-year-old sister May was happily rolling around in a mud puddle. "Wook at me, I'm a widdew piggy!" she exclaimed. "Piggies wuv mud! Oink-oink!" It was hard to imagine that her frilly dress had been bright purple just moments earlier.

"The door," Katie pleaded. "Hurry, Ashley-Rose!"

Clunk, clunk, clunk! The racecar flew out of Patrick's hand, bumpety-bump-bumped across the driveway and skidded into the grass. Shrieks from the boys followed and they both dove at once to get the toy.

May joyfully skipped over to her brothers and tumbled on top of them. She wrapped her slimy, dripping, muddy arms around them. "Thwee-way hug!" she said with an enormous grin. Jingles woofed and jumped onto the pile of kids, making it a four-way hug.

"WAAAAAAAAAA!!!" the baby wailed louder, "WAAAAAAAAA!" Her mouth formed a gigantic O, giving a clear view all the way from her only two teeth down to her tonsils.

"You *do* have the key, don't you?" Katie said to me.

I'm pretty good at reading body language (that's how people show their feelings by the way they move their hands, head or body). Katie's body language (hands thrown up in the air) was saying: "Oh no, don't tell me you don't have the key."

There was no need to tell her. She knew all too well about my habit of rushing rushing rushing, only to bungle* things and make big mistakes.

"Really Ashley-Rose," she groaned, "sometimes you're more of a *hassle** than a *helper*!"

13

Chapter Two

THE LUCKY LIST

Looking down at the three muddy kids, barking dog and crying baby, I knew that Katie was right.

The truth hurt—a lot. My eyes stung and began to fill with tears.

In my excitement to hurry outside and play with the kids, I had goofed things up for the umpteenth* time.

No one would ever let me forget the time I put little Marie Willabee's baby doll in the freezer and the strawberry swirl ice cream in her toy chest. The ice cream melted into a sticky, soupy mess, and the doll's braids froze standing straight up from her head.

And I will never live down the sizzling hot summer day that I did a cannonball into the Clapdoodle's pool. I was so excited to go swimming that I completely forgot I was still wearing my school uniform. I was rushing then, too.

14

I peeked quickly again through the window, as if the Dotts' house key might have magically disappeared from the table and would reappear in my pocket. It hadn't.

I guess you could say it was my key to happiness. Locking the door, being responsible for the key and helping get the kids back inside the house safely would have shown Katie that I'd learned the lessons we'd covered in the Junior Babysitters training class called

"Safety for Kids." And that would have earned a pink bead for my Babysitting Bracelet.

Here's how it works: I can earn a bead by helping out one of the NSB members on a job and showing I've learned three skills that were taught in a Juniors class.

Once I've earned 15 pink beads, they will be strung on a special Babysitting Bracelet. It's a huge honor for a Junior to earn a bracelet because it's a symbol* of accomplishments. I couldn't wait!

I saw Katie and the Dott kids huddling under a tree, trying to get shelter from the pouring rain. There would be no bead for me today, that was for sure.

"I have a great idea," I said, pointing my finger up into the air.

"You and your great ideas," Katie muttered* under her breath.

"I'll hunt around and see if the Dotts hid a key somewhere," I said hopefully.

I looked under the doormat, flowerpots and a cement bunny on the porch. Strands of hair clung across my wet face in an annoying way. I pawed them away and my fingers left dirty splotches all over my nose and forehead. *Who looks like a "widdew piggy" now?* I thought.

I got down on my hands and knees, crawled around bushes and searched for one of those fake gray rocks that are hollow* in the middle and hold a key.

As I rustled around under a big flowering bush, I heard bits and pieces of what Katie was saying, "…about what I said…I didn't mean it, Ashley-Rose…sorry…"

She felt bad that she had made *me* feel bad. She's 15 years old and like a big sister to me. I knew that she wouldn't hurt my feelings on purpose.

The next-door neighbor, Mrs. Rise, spotted our drenched* group. Mrs. Rise is known by the kids on Nickel Street as Mrs. Spies. She is always sitting on her porch, moving back and forth on a creaky rocking chair and craning her neck every which way to see what we are up to.

That's where she was right then, and that's exactly what she was doing. But she was also waving something around in the air.

"I have an extra key!" she screeched across the yard. "The Dotts gave it to me so I can water their plants when they go on vacation. You can borrow it but you'll have to give it right back to me."

Thank goodness for nosy neighbors!

ის ის

Once inside the house, we got the kids changed into clean, dry clothes. Katie gave Violet a much-needed bottle while I played hide-and-seek with Jack, Patrick and May.

I hid in a dark closet and waited to be discovered by May, who was "It." Sitting on a lumpy pile of what felt like baseball mitts and balls, I let out a long sad sigh. I'd really had my heart set on earning a bead.

I made a Lucky List in my mind. My mom got me started doing this when I was little, to focus on the good stuff in my life. She says that even when times are tough, there are still things to be thankful for.

Top 10 Reasons I'm Lucky

#1: My cousin Katie lives right next door to me on Nickel Street. How cool is that!

#2: Even though I'm not an NSB member yet, I get to attend their Bagels-and-Babysitting Breakfast Meetings every Saturday in Katie's kitchen. That happens to be the day Katie "watches" me while my mother works as a nurse at the hospital.

All six of the NSB are best friends. It's easy to remember everyone in their club because their names all begin with the letter K: Katie, Kelly, Karla, Karen, Kim and Kristin.

#3: I'm the NSB Secretary! Maybe they were half joking when they gave me the title of Secretary, but it stuck—and I'm proud of it. While the girls are discussing their babysitting schedules at the breakfast meeting, I write down every detail in my pocket-sized notebook and calendar.

I keep track of who is babysitting for which family, the times and the dates. I record who has softball/guitar/dance/gymnastics/drama practice and when.

And I jot down who can't babysit on certain days because they're getting new braces or going to their grandma's house for dinner or studying for a test.

#4: The Junior Babysitters club is so so so so so much fun. Each month the NSB holds a Juniors class about a babysitting subject such as "Safety for Kids," "Baby's Bath Time" and "Bedtime Routines."

#5: My friends are Juniors, too, including my bestest-best friend Jules.

#6: I've already earned 2 beads for my Babysitting Bracelet. That's impressive.

#7: The NSB decorated T-shirts and babysitting bags with a heart and JB club logo*! They gave one of each to every Junior.

I use my bag to carry my "Being a Babysitter from A to Z" Book, my Junior Babysitters club membership card, my pocket-sized notebook and calendar, and a pink pen.

I also bring construction paper, markers, a sing-along book, a pink bunny hand puppet with silly button eyes (so cute!), stickers and games to amuse the kids we babysit.

#8: I get to wear my JB club T-shirt when I'm helping out at babysitting jobs.

#9: The Nickel Street neighborhood is a blast. It's shaped like the number "8" with a lollipop stick on the bottom. Tons of babies, toddlers, and boys and girls of all ages live here so there's always something interesting happening.

#10: May opened the door and "found" me. Hooray! I can finally get out of the dark closet!

Chapter Three

CAN YOU HEAR ME NOW?

"Sorry I'm late!" I exclaimed to the six members of the NSB as I dashed into Katie's house on Saturday morning. In my rush, I stumbled on the edge of the rug.

I grunted as I took a spill onto the floor. "Ooomph!" I looked around. Everyone saw me. How embarrassing!

Katie looked concerned. "Are you okay?"

"Slow down, Zoom," laughed Kim.

Zoom is the nickname the NSB calls me when I'm zipping around at high speed. They complain that sometimes I have *way* too much energy. But my mother says she wishes she could have even half of my energy.

The NSB also grumbles that I have *way* too many so-called great ideas. They make it sound like having a lot of suggestions is a bad thing.

Honestly! I thought. *Sometimes they treat me like an annoying little sister!*

"Did I miss anything?" I asked. I plunked myself down on my Junior Babysitters club chair in the corner of the kitchen and tried to catch my breath.

I fumbled around inside my JB bag and took out my pocket-sized JB notebook and calendar and pink pen.

The wonderful smell of cinnamon bagels baking filled the room. Katie's mom, my Aunt Barb, makes them every Saturday morning for the NSB. Katie, Kelly, Karen, Kim, Karla and Kristin were all gathered at the dining table.

"Now that the *Secretary* has arrived, let's begin the meeting," said Kelly with a smile.

"First let's tell Zoom the good news," Karen joked, "you know, how the NSB was just about to promote* her."

"Really?" I said.

"To a *key** position in the NSB," teased Karla.

"Maybe Chief Keeper of the *Keys*," added Kristin.

"Or even Chief *Lock*smith," said Karen.

I scowled*. "Very funny. Did I miss anything that I should write down?" But no one heard me. They were all giggling among themselves.

How can I get them to take me seriously as a Junior Babysitter and realize I'm not a little kid anymore? I wondered. *Maybe my new idea will wow them.* This idea wasn't just great, it was downright fabulous!

I spoke in a loud voice to get their attention. "I have a fabulous idea. It's a kids'—"

Kelly cut me off. "Ashley-Rose, we're in the middle of the NSB meeting right now. How about if you finish rolling the coins?"

Not the coins again! I thought. Last year the NSB

decided to raise money for a kids' charity and I've been rolling coins ever since.

I guess I have no one to blame but myself. It was my suggestion that, since they are the Nickel Street Babysitters, they could donate a nickel from every dollar they earned on babysitting jobs.

They loved the idea but did I get any credit for it? Not a chance. In fact, usually when I open my mouth to make a suggestion, they act a bit irritated, roll their eyes or smirk*.

They bring their coins to the Saturday meeting and drop them into a pink-and-silver Nickel Jar.

Then one of the girls hands me the Nickel Jar and asks me to put the coins in brown paper tube-shaped wrappers. Once they are all rolled, and there is a good amount of money, the NSB will take the rolls of coins to the bank and exchange them for paper money.

Then the babysitters and Juniors will buy backpacks and school supplies. There's a group at the hospital where my mom works that will give them to kids whose families can't afford them.

Rolling coins while taking good notes is nearly impossible.

"Sure," I said, "but can I tell you my fabulous idea first?" No one heard me because they were listening to Katie announce everyone's schedules for the coming week.

I sat cross-legged on the carpet, quietly rolled coins and hastily* scribbled notes.

"The Swansons need a babysitter on Thursday night from 5:00 to 7:00 p.m.," Katie said. "I know that Karla, Kim and Kristin all have a track meet that night. I can't do it because I'm already babysitting for the Jenkins' kids."

"I have a dentist appointment," said Kelly.

"And I have a math test the next day, so I'll be studying,"

said Karen.

"That's too bad," said Katie. "It looks like we'll have to turn down the babysitting job since everyone is busy."

My ears perked up. *Not everyone is busy*, I thought. *This is my big chance to really help the NSB and to prove I'm responsible, too.*

"No need to cancel," I shouted. "I have a great idea!"

Chapter Four

THE LAST ONE PICKED

I hopped to my feet and coins rolled in every direction. "*I'm* free on Thursday night! *I* can babysit for the Swanson kids!"

The body language of the NSB (a frown, a sigh, a snicker, a head shaking "no") said this idea wasn't a winner.

"Ashley-Rose," said Katie gently, "you can't babysit by yourself just yet."

"But I've already earned two beads in the Junior Babysitters club," I insisted.

"You know the rules, Ashley-Rose," said Kristin. "When you finish all the classes, earn your bracelet and you're older, you'll be ready to babysit."

"Right now you're still learning and growing up," said Kim.

Growing up, shmowing up! I thought. *It's taking forever to grow up!*

"I have lots of experience with kids," I said. "Think about all the babysitting jobs I've helped out at!" I looked around. No nods of agreement. No smiles.

I pressed on, "I've fetched diapers, played peek-a-boo with the babies, and sung every song in the sing-a-long book twice until Jack and Patrick fell asleep. I've had my hair done in 26 ponytails by tiny hands that yank and tug.

"And I've been buried in the sandbox from head to toe. Sand in your pants is NOT comfortable."

The NSB didn't hear me (again!). Katie was reading out loud the upcoming jobs she had listed in her datebook. It's about the size of a paperback book and has a page for each day of the year.

I knew I might as well be talking to myself when I grumbled, "Think about how many hours I've spent pretending I'm a unicorn, fairy, firefighter, tightrope walker, walrus, president, barber, gopher and magician. I'm an expert in the land of make-believe.

"I know all the kids' favorite colors, foods, numbers, dolls, socks and riddles. I've—"

Oh never mind. It was no use. *Sometimes it stinks being eight years old,* I thought, as I scurried around gathering coins. *No one listens to me.*

Near the end of the meeting, Katie said, "The only thing left to discuss is which Junior Babysitter you would like to have help you tonight."

Since it was the weekend, it was a busy night for babysitting jobs. Everyone quickly shouted out the name of a Junior.

"I get Alana!" "Jules can come with me!" "I call Kerry!" and so on.

31

Slow down, I thought. *It's hard to write these names down so fast in my notebook.* I studied the list. The girls had shouted out all the Juniors' names. All except mine.

"Ooooooh-kaaaaaay," Katie said slowly. She twitched her mouth to the left and then right. "I guess Ashley-Rose will, um, help me."

She must have noticed the enormous disappointment that was written all over my face, because suddenly she changed her tune*. "Yeah, that's awesome. Ashley-Rose will help me babysit the Dotts again."

✥ ✥

The Juniors arrived a few minutes before the NSB meeting ended and the Babysitters "Baby's Bath Time" training class began.

Katie handed out a thick piece of bright yellow paper. She read each of the sentences aloud and then we discussed them.

Important Rules for Bath Time:

1. NEVER LEAVE A BABY OR A SMALL CHILD ALONE IN A BATHTUB. NOT EVEN FOR A FEW SECONDS; NOT TO ANSWER THE PHONE, THE DOOR—NOT AT ALL!!

2. ONLY GIVE A BABY OR SMALL CHILD A BATH IF YOU ARE A CERTIFIED BABYSITTER, MEANING YOU HAVE TAKEN A COURSE OR CLASS AND RECEIVED APPROVAL AFTER THE COURSE OR CLASS.

3. ONLY GIVE A BABY OR SMALL CHILD A BATH IF THE PARENT ASKS YOU TO DO SO.

The NSB gave us a doll to practice on that was the same size as a real baby.

"First," said Kim, "put all the items you'll need for bath time beside you, because you will always want to have one hand supporting the baby."

We set the soft baby towel and baby shampoo beside the doll-sized bathtub. Then we added a little bit of water to the small tub. Karen showed us how to poke our elbows into the water to make sure the temperature was not too hot or too cold. We took turns bathing the baby doll, drying her and putting on her pajamas.

That night, I helped Katie give Violet a real bath. May, Patrick and Jack were brushing Jingles in the hallway where we could keep an eye on them.

Violet happily played with her turtle and whale tub toys. She sputtered and blinked when Katie washed the baby shampoo out of her hair.

Afterwards, Katie wrapped Violet in a cozy-soft pink towel with a kitty face and whiskers on the hood, and I patted her dry. Katie let me help put Violet's pajamas on, just like we'd practiced.

"Congratulations!" Katie said. "You just earned your bead for the 'Baby's Bath Time' class."

I will treasure that bead because I can't think of anything cuter than Violet with her almost-toothless grin splashing around with her tub toys.

⚜ ⚜

A few minutes later I found out that I had to have my tonsils removed. I was also told that I had a terrible-awful-very-high fever, a major headache, an ear infection in both ears and chicken pox.

I was lying on my back on a shaggy rug in the Dotts' family room and getting a whole bunch of medical tests.

Dr. Jack shook his head sadly. "You'd also better talk to Dr. Patrick," he said, patting my head. "I'm afraid your heart sounds weird."

Violet crawled over my stomach to get her ball, leaving a powerful smell in her trail.

"Pea-yewww!" cried May, holding her nose.

Dr. Patrick paid no attention to the stink and kept listening to my heart. He took his stethoscope out of his ears and looked serious. "You might have to stay in this hospital for a month."

"Oh dear," I said. "Are you sure, Doctor?"

"I'm positive," he said, wagging his finger at me. For another twenty minutes there were more tests and more bad news about my health. The kids put a cast on my leg made of toilet paper, drew bandages on my elbow with washable markers and gave me pretend shots in both arms.

But the good news was that while I was pretending to be the patient, I *wasn't* dealing with that stinky diaper! Poor Katie. Thank goodness diaper changing is strictly off-limits for Juniors.

꿈 꿈

A couple of weeks later at Katie's house, the NSB held a babysitting class for the Juniors on "Activities for Every Age."

We learned that tiny babies mostly need to be held, cuddled and fed. Toddlers like stacking blocks, pushing buttons to make lights flash or music play, and being very, very busy.

Kids who are a little older like board games, sports, art projects, imagination games, reading books, telling stories and sometimes they're happiest just showing you every single thing in their bedrooms.

"In order to earn your next bead," said Kelly, "the Juniors must come up with a Friday night activity. It must be free, fun and appropriate for all the ages of the kids we babysit. Then you can help plan the activity."

Kim nodded her head. "The NSB will be in the living room planning the next babysitting class. We'll be back in twenty minutes to hear your very best Friday night activity."

There was an excited buzz* around the table. All my friends took turns shouting out ideas. I jotted them down in my notebook.

"A carnival!" "A picnic!" "Miniature golf!" "Flashlight tag!" "A block party!"

There were many suggestions but none of them was exactly what the NSB had asked for: free, fun and appropriate for all the ages of the kids we babysit.

The body language of my friends showed that everyone was out of ideas.

Jules was tracing the daisies on the tablecloth with her finger. Kerry was gazing out the window at nothing in particular. Alana's elbows were on the table and her hands were smushing her cheeks and giving herself fish lips. Lizzie was peeling a grape with no intention of eating it. Tess was twisting a long piece of hair around her finger.

I drummed my fingers on my chin. I squinted my

eyes and thought harder.

A kite-flying contest? Too old for the babies. A baby-crawling race? Too young for the six-year-olds. Tie-dying T-shirts? Planting a garden? Charades? A parade? A talent show? A knot-tying class? No. No. And more nos.

Although we were all quiet and concentrating, it was surprisingly noisy. I heard the fridge hum. Katie's dog, Butterscotch, scratched his neck with his hind* leg and the metal tags on his collar jingled. Jules's chair creaked when she unfolded her legs. A car door slammed outside.

I clasped my hands on top of my head. *There's an idea somewhere in this noggin* of mine,* I thought. *All I need is one fabulous idea to help earn my bead.*

Chapter Five

THE FABULOUS IDEA

Suddenly that fabulous idea I'd had all along bubbled out of me. "How about a Jukebox Party?" I asked.

I gazed around the table to see what the reaction was. Ten eyes lit up.

"It could be held in Katie's garage," I continued. "She has a jukebox and wait until you see it!"

"What's a jukebox?" asked Tess.

"It's a big machine this high that plays music," I said, using my hand to show a height in the air that was about as tall as I am.

I continued explaining, "Each song title has a number next to it. When you push the numbered buttons, the jukebox plays the song you selected. Hers has yellow and orange and green lights that flash. The kids will love it."

All my friends were excited, but when we told the NSB, they weren't as enthusiastic.

"There's three years' worth of dust and cobwebs in the garage," Katie said.

My Aunt Barb was in the kitchen washing dishes. "Gee, it would be *wonderful* to get that jukebox going again!"

Her body language (both hands, covered in rubber gloves and suds, crossed on her heart) said she missed hearing the jukebox playing music.

Katie looked doubtful. "I don't know. It sounds like a lot of work to clean up the garage. Boxes are everywhere."

"It's about time I got rid of those boxes of old junk anyway," said Aunt Barb.

"We'll do all the cleaning, we promise," the Juniors cried. "Please, please, pleeeeeeeeeease?"

"Before you make any promises," Katie said, "come on out and see for yourself what a huge mess it is."

We all scrambled out of our chairs and headed to the driveway.

Jules used her sleeve to clear a circle on the dusty garage window. Standing on our tiptoes, we took turns peeking inside. We couldn't see much because boxes were blocking the windows.

Katie unlocked the squeaky door and everyone crowded in at once. It was hot and dim* and stuffy* inside.

Suddenly there was a blare* of lively music. Bright, colorful lights flashed in every direction.

All the Juniors rushed around a wall of stacked boxes to the corner where Katie, Kelly, Kim, Karla, Karen and Kristin were already gathered in front of the jukebox. Katie was pushing square buttons on the front.

"Play #128, 'Dixie Jig'!" Kelly said, pointing to the glass in front of the jukebox where the songs were listed. "I love that song!"

"Oooh, ooh, ooh, play #305 next!" shouted Karla.

Everyone was calling out their song picks at once. "#161!" "#312!" "#177!"

The lights on the jukebox glowed, the music played and the NSB and Juniors danced and laughed.

Underneath all this junk and cobwebs, I thought, *is the best party place ever.*

"I have a great idea," I said. Ignoring someone's groan, I plowed on, "Let's call this the Jukebox Clubhouse."

Jules pointed to one corner of the garage. "We could put kid-sized tables and chairs over there. I'm sure it will be okay with my dad if we use the ones in our attic."

Kerry piped up, "I have some we can use, too."

Alana stood in the middle of the garage. "And the dance floor can be right here."

Tess looked up at the ceiling. "I have a whole bunch of bright green, purple and blue streamers left over from my birthday party. Let's hang them from the rafters*."

"Hmmm," said Karla. "Just a thought…maybe once the garage is spruced* up, we can have the Junior Babysitters classes here, too."

In the end, the NSB agreed that the Juniors could be in charge of planning and leading the Friday Jukebox Party and the NSB would be there as the babysitters.

It was decided that the first party would be in three weeks. It would be held early so the kids wouldn't be out much past their usual bedtimes.

"You know, Ashley-Rose," said Karen, "your idea to turn the garage into the Jukebox Clubhouse isn't half bad." A couple of the other NSB members nodded.

I'm pretty sure that's a compliment, I thought. *Not half bad means it's half good, right?* Considering my history of babysitting bloopers, even half of a compliment seemed better than none at all.

With the NSB's help, the Juniors made a checklist of the things we would need to do: clean the garage, baby-proof it (make the garage safe for babies and toddlers), decorate, plan activities and games to keep the kids entertained, and make fliers to spread the word.

We decided what the fliers should say and the Juniors used the last fifteen minutes of class to make them. I took the construction paper and markers out of my Junior Babysitters bag and slid them to the middle of the table so everyone could reach them.

Hey kids, you're invited to the
Nickel Street
♪♪Jukebox Party♫
Dance, sing and play musical games.
Fun Fun Fun for kids of all ages!

5:30–7:30 p.m.
First Friday of the Month
in the newly decorated
Jukebox Clubhouse
(Katie's garage)

No babysitting fee.
Donations will buy backpacks &
school supplies for kids in need.
Planned by the Junior Babysitters.
Supervised by the NSB.
Please RSVP* to Katie.

Chapter Six

JILLY WANTS A DILLY

Right after the NSB Bagels-and-Babysitting Breakfast Meeting the next Saturday, the Juniors met at Katie's garage to start cleaning it up. The NSB brought rags, buckets of sudsy water, sponges, scrub brushes, trash bags and brooms.

My Aunt Barb had taken all of the boxes out of the garage and was sorting her stuff into four piles: Keep, Give Away, Throw Away and Recycle.

Katie wasn't kidding when she said her garage was a big mess. Boy was it!

We swept, vacuumed and mopped the floor. We oiled the squeaky door. We dusted and scrubbed and washed windows. And the whole time, we hummed and sang along to songs on the jukebox.

When we finished, we were hot and sweaty but the Jukebox Clubhouse looked spotless and smelled fresh. The Juniors went outside and flopped down on the grass. Aunt Barb brought us a jug of apple cider, which we gulped down in less than a minute.

"Let's play Musical Chairs at the Jukebox Party," Jules suggested.

"What else should we play?" asked Kerry. "How about Freeze Dance?"

"What's Freeze Dance?" wondered Alana.

"You've never played Freeze Dance?!" the rest of us chorused*.

I explained, "While a song is playing, you dance. And when the music is suddenly stopped, you have to 'freeze' in whatever position you're in."

"It's hilarious!" Lizzie hooted.

"We could also give out awards that celebrate good things that the kids do," I said. "They could earn them for getting homework done on time or keeping their bedrooms clean."

"Maybe one for sharing toys," said Tess. "That's a biggie with kids."

"And eating their veggies," suggested Alana.

"And for the toddlers, new skills like saying a word or using a spoon for the first time," said Jules.

"Every child should get an award, so each person feels special," Kerry said.

We decided to ask the parents to be on the lookout for good behavior, too.

That night was another busy Saturday night for the NSB. All the babysitters had jobs.

Katie walked with me to the Clapdoodle's house, where I was going to help Karla babysit six-year-old Marybeth and her four-year-old sister Jillian (whose nickname is Jilly).

Karla asked them what they'd like to do before she gave them dinner.

"I have a great idea," I said.

"I'm sure you do," said Karla with a smile.

"How about if we look for lucky four-leaf clovers?" I knew a green patch in the park across the street where four-leaf clovers sometimes grow.

"Yippee!" shouted Jillian, running around in circles. "Jilly loves lucky clovers!"

"Can we press them in between wax paper like we did with the leaves?" Marybeth asked. "Then we can hang them in the window?"

"You betcha!" I said. "If it's okay with Karla, that is."

"Sure, let's go," Karla said.

"First," I said to the girls, "you have to hold my hand and we'll look both ways before we cross the street."

"Congratulations," Karla said to me.

I had no idea what she was talking about.

"Ashley-Rose, you're on your way to earning your bead for the 'Safety for Kids' class!" She explained, "You used two of the lessons you learned." She held up one finger, then two fingers, "One, holding kids' hands, and two, teaching them to look both ways before crossing the street."

I was beaming, inside and out.

After each of the girls found a lucky clover

we rolled over onto our backs and did a little cloud watching.

"Look at that cloud," I said. "It looks like a giraffe. See its long neck?"

"I see it, too," said Karla. "It even has spots."

Marybeth waved her clover in the direction of a puffy white cloud that appeared to be wearing a crown. "That one looks like a king!"

Jillian pointed, "There's a princess! Princess Jilly!"

Princess Jilly was everywhere. Jillian imagined that the crack on her bedroom ceiling looked like the princess. She drew pictures of her with sidewalk chalk. And once she smushed her mashed potatoes around on her plate to look like Princess Jilly.

❧ ☙

Later on, I helped Karla get the kids' dinner ready. One thing I've noticed is that kids can get crabby when they're hungry or tired. Marybeth and Jillian were both hungry *and* tired.

While we were cutting pears into bite-sized pieces, we played Can You Name That Song? Karla and

I took turns whistling tunes and they guessed the names. But they quickly became impatient.

"Where's my orange juice?" demanded Marybeth, clanging her spoon on her plate.

"I'm pouring your orange juice right now, honey," Karla said in a gentle voice.

"Can I have a dill pickle?" cried Jillian. "Mommy said I could have a dill pickle tonight!"

She was about to throw a temper tantrum. "I'll get you a pickle, Jilly," I said.

I rummaged* through the fridge and was relieved to see two fat dill pickles in a clear plastic jar that was shaped like a miniature* barrel. Unfortunately the pickles were stuck sideways and tightly wedged in the bottom.

I thumped the jar with the palm of my hand to try to set them free. I stabbed them quickly with a fork to get them out but it didn't work. The strong-smelling pickle juice splashed all over my Junior Babysitters T-shirt and spilled onto the kitchen floor.

"Slow down, Zoom. Take it easy with that fork," Karla advised. "Remember the rules we learned in the 'Safety for Kids' class? Rushing leads to mistakes."

"JILLY WANTS A DILLY, JILLY WANTS A DILLY!" chanted Jillian.

The louder she screeched, the harder I tried to get the pickles unstuck.

"Do you want some help?" Karla asked.

I shook my head. I was determined to get that pickle out.

"WHERE'S MY PICKLE?!" hollered Jillian, then "I WANT MY MOMMY!"

Quickly I wiggled my fingers around in the jar, but they were not quite long enough to get a grip on the pickles. I inched my knuckles inside, then my whole hand.

Success! I grabbed a pickle.

But uh-oh! My hand was stuck!

I twisted the jar around and around leaving a red ring on my wrist. I squished my fingers together and tried to wriggle my hand out. Lifting my hand up in the air, pickle jar and all, I stared at it and wondered, *How did I get in this situation anyway?*

Oh yes. Rushing. That's how.

Jillian stopped shouting and started giggling. Marybeth laughed so hard the orange juice sprayed out of her mouth and all over the table.

It was a funny sight to them, but I was filled with fear. Would I still earn my "Safety for Kids" bead? Would I have to spend the rest of my life like this?

My future flashed before my eyes: I saw myself trying to play tennis with Jules, a racket in one hand and a pickle jar weighing down my other.

I imagined myself at the NSB Bagels-and-Babysitting Breakfast Meeting, taking notes with one hand and the other hand inside the pickle jar with a bunch of coins clinking around.

Then my mind fast-forwarded a few years to when I would be old enough to babysit on my own. In my imagination, I was feeding a baby with one hand. On the other hand was my Babysitting Bracelet, clearly visible inside the pickle jar!

Seriously, who would hire a babysitter with a pickle jar permanently stuck on her hand? No one!

My dream, down the drain! I thought. *My life is ruined!*

Chapter Seven

NOT REALLY

The girls were jiggling with laughter. Marybeth fell off her chair and was rolling around on the floor holding her stomach.

Out of the corner of my eye, I noticed that Karla was not amused. Not one bit.

Her body language (hands on her hips and head shaking slowly from side to side) said she wasn't surprised I'd just made another one of my flubs.

Then more body language (with her pointer finger) said, "Come to the sink, Zoom." She held my hand over the sink and dripped dishwashing soap all around the rim of the plastic pickle jar.

"Gently, gently," she said, sliding my hand ever so slowly out of the jar.

I held up my hand and looked at it, amazed. "Wow," I gasped, "how did you know how to do that?"

"Last year my sister tried on a ring that was too small," Karla said. "She used soap to slither her finger out of the ring. Soap works like magic because it makes everything slippery."

"I have a great idea," I said.

"Uh-oh," replied Karla. "What is it?"

I pointed in two directions: the dining table and the kitchen floor. "How about if I clean up all that orange juice and all this smelly pickle juice?"

"Now *that* is a great idea," said Karla.

Before bedtime, I got a pink-and-gold jewelry box out of my Junior Babysitters bag. It's filled with all kinds of treasures and I tell the kids it's my Not Really Treasure Trove*.

I make up all kinds of silly stories about the objects. The kids get a big kick out of them.

Marybeth held up a glittering white pinecone. "Where did you get this?"

"Oh, Santa Claus gave that to me to say thank you for helping him brush the reindeer," I said.

"*Really?*" Marybeth asked.

I chuckled*. "Not really."

Jillian pointed to a long necklace with big colorful beads that looked like they came from a gumball machine. Karla took it out of the box and slipped it around Jillian's neck.

"A beautiful Queen gave me those precious jewels to wear to a *very* grand party at the Gumball Palace," I whispered.

Both of the girls' eyes were big and wide. "*Really?*" They both said at once.

"Not really," I grinned.

Marybeth held a clear crystal bear up to the light. As she turned it this way and that, it sparkled with many colors. I told the little girls that once upon a time a polar bear was bored with being plain white so he asked a rainbow if he could borrow its pretty colors.

"*Really?*" they asked.

"Not really," I said.

They bounced a ball that's made from a "million-trillion-gazillion" red, yellow, blue and green rubber bands. "Once it bounced all the way to Mars and back!"

"*Really?*" they said.

"Not really," I said.

The Clapdoodle's doorbell rang at 7:22 p.m. I knew it was my mom who had come to pick me up. Karla went to answer the door. For safety reasons, only NSB are allowed to open the door.

I started packing everything back up in my box. "It's time for me to go now—and time for you to go to bed."

The girls groaned. "Not really?" they said hopefully. They were sad I was leaving.

"Yes, really," I said, giving them each a goodnight hug.

"I like you, even when you smell like a dill pickle," Marybeth said with a yawn.

Jillian rubbed her eyes. "*Especially* when you smell like a dill pickle."

∽ ∾

On Sunday I began to fret. *What if no one came to the Jukebox Party? Or what if kids came but didn't have fun?*

My mom said that's called pre-party jitters and it's a perfectly normal feeling when you're planning a party. I didn't have much chance to worry, because it was time to meet the Juniors and NSB at the Jukebox Clubhouse.

The Juniors decided that each of us would plan and lead one party activity for 15 minutes. Everyone signed up for the activity they wanted to be in charge of.

I made a schedule and hung it on the garage wall.

<u>*Jukebox Party Schedule of Events*</u>
5:30 Kids Arrive
5:45 Musical Chairs (Jules)
6:00 Hokey Pokey (Alana)
6:15 Sing-Along (Tess)
6:30 Freeze Dance (Kerry)
6:45 Dance Contest (Lizzie)

61

7:00 *Awards (Ashley-Rose)*
7:15 *Clean-up Song (everyone picks up)*
7:30 *Parents Arrive*

Jules and Kerry arranged the little tables and chairs in one corner. Tess put sing-along songbooks on the tables. Lizzie and I made posters decorated with huge musical notes in bold colors, and Alana hung them on the wall.

My mom climbed a stepladder and taped streamers to the rafters.

Aunt Barb had found a disco ball in one of her boxes and she hung it from a light in the garage. It was covered with tiny square mirrors. As it spun, it created a blizzard of little white lights that whirled around on the walls.

"I have to leave for gymnastics practice," said Kelly, as she ran a hairbrush through her long, silky brown hair. "But I just want to say this Clubhouse rocks! Way to go, Juniors."

I reached for Kelly's hairbrush. "You just gave me a great idea."

Kelly groaned, but I could detect a laugh.

"Kids love to pretend they're in a band," I said. "How about if the kids used things like hairbrushes or bananas as make-believe microphones for singing?" I held the "microphone" up to my lips and began lip-syncing to the song that was playing on the jukebox.

Kerry grabbed a broom that was leaning against the wall and strummed it like a guitar.

"My mom always gave us big plastic containers with lids to beat like drums," said Tess, "and wooden spoons as drumsticks. I can bring those."

"I'll bring frying pan lids to use as cymbals*," said Jules.

We set up another corner of the garage as the band area. Karen had brought a round shaggy blue rug from her bedroom and Alana made a poster that said "Clubhouse Stage."

"By the way, how many kids are signed up to come on Friday night?" I asked.

The NSB gave each other nervous looks. "We didn't want to tell you," Katie hesitated. "There's a little problem."

"Now don't get upset," said Kim.

"It's not that big of a deal," said Karen.

"We're sure everything will work out fine," added Karla.

The Juniors exchanged worried glances.

"Has *anyone* signed up yet?" I asked. "Anyone at all?"

Chapter Eight

THE WAITING LIST

"That's the problem," said Karen.

"There isn't anyone who *didn't* sign up," said Katie.

"There's actually a waiting list!" Kim added. "All of the families we babysit for wanted to sign their kids up for the Jukebox Party. Unfortunately the garage won't safely hold that many kids at once."

"A waiting list?" I was so excited.

"Yes, the Tylers' three boys and the Kents' daughter are on the waiting list in case other families cancel," Karla said.

Karen explained, "The parents are thrilled that they can go out for a couple of hours on Friday, have dinner or get a few errands done. And they love the idea that donations will be used to help a kids' charity."

"Okay everybody, this coming Saturday is a Big Day," said Katie. Her body language (using two fingers

64

on each hand to put quote marks around Big Day) said, "This is important."

"It's the Junior Babysitters class, 'Indoor Fun and Games.' We'll cover all kinds of crafts, games and activities to keep kids entertained on rainy days. This class is the best one yet, so don't miss it."

<hr />

"I'm sorry for the short notice," I overheard my mother say a few days later. She was talking on the phone to the head nurse at the hospital. "I won't be able to work tomorrow because Ashley-Rose has the flu."

The next day was the Big Day (a Saturday), and it meant that I would miss out on three things: 1) being the Secretary at the NSB meeting, 2) going to the best Junior Babysitters training class yet and 3) babysitting the Dotts with Kim (which would be a chance to earn the bead I'd lost during the pickle problem).

I felt miserable. I pulled the covers up over my head.

My mother tiptoed into my room and set a tray on my nightstand.

Even though my eyes were closed, I knew exactly what was on the tray: a plate with five saltine crackers and a glass of fizzy ginger ale with lots of ice and a bendable straw. That's what she always brings me when I'm sick.

Before she tiptoed back out of the room she whispered, "I'm sorry you feel terrible. And it stinks that you will miss the meeting and the class tomorrow. But I bet you could still think of plenty of things to put on your Lucky List."

I doubted it. But maybe I could manage to come up with a "mini" Lucky List.

Top 5 Reasons I'm Lucky

#1: I think my nose is just the right size (so phooey to the boys at school who call me Ashley-Nose).

#2: My cat, Slowpoke, is purring, and that makes me feel happy.

#3: My bedroom is the color of the inside of a ripe watermelon and that's my favorite color.

#4: I will not have to roll coins tomorrow.

#5: I have a snuggly blanket, soft pillow and (yawn)....

When I awoke the next morning I felt a little perkier and was even able to stomach a few nibbles of toast. I propped my pillows up, leaned back and started thinking about awards for the Jukebox Party. I pulled my construction paper and markers from my Junior Babysitters bag.

I came up with an award for each of the kids we

babysit, even the kids who couldn't be at the party.

The Super-Duper Sharing Awards went to Jack and Patrick, who had made a deal with each other to trade their racecars every other day.

The Queen of Veggies Award was for Marybeth, who finished her peas and carrots at dinner one night—and discovered she actually likes them.

The Ace Student Award went to Stanley Swanson, who did his homework every day after school for a week without being reminded.

On Sunday, I felt tiptop. My mom declared that I was now germ-free. "You can go outside and play if you want to."

The phone rang and it was Katie. She was calling to see how I was feeling.

"Good as new," I said, "but I missed being with the NSB yesterday."

"No sweat," said Katie, "Take this week off from your secretarial duties."

It stung* that she did not say they missed me, too.

"I'd *never ever* do that," I insisted. "Can I come over and check out what's new on the babysitting schedule?"

"All right." She sighed heavily, like I had just asked her to roll coins or some other boring chore. "I know how you like to know everything that goes on in the meetings. I'm leaving to go to the movies, but my mom is here having lunch with the Clapdoodles if you want to stop by. I'll leave my datebook on my bed."

"Thanks, Katie," I said. "And by the way, I really missed being with the Dott kids last night, too."

"Well there's nothing you can do about getting sick," she replied.

Nobody missed me? Not even the Dott kids?

"Does anybody need a Junior to help them this week?" I asked.

"Well, as a matter of fact, Mrs. Swanson called this morning to see if anyone could babysit today from 2:00 to 3:30 p.m.," Katie said. "Kelly is going to babysit."

"Can I help? Please?" I begged.

"If you really think you're up to it," she said.

Oh, I really think I'm up to it all right, I thought. I'd finally get the chance to earn my pink bead. *Wa-hoo!*

69

Chapter Nine

THE CAT'S PAJAMAS

The Nickel Street Jukebox Party was a whopping success!

Many of the kids had never seen a jukebox. They thought the bright lights and music were the cat's pajamas (in other words, fantastic).

The kids were so cute pretending they were in a band, and they really got into it. Freeze Dance was hilarious. The Dance Contest and Sing-Along were huge hits. Everyone, from our youngest Jukebox Party guest to our oldest, had a blast.

Jules took lots of photos so that we could print them out and hang them on the Jukebox Clubhouse bulletin board.

The NSB were the babysitters, but they let the Juniors be in charge of almost everything. When the parents came at 7:30, some kids didn't want to go home. That's how much fun it was.

"Can we stay with the Jukebox Babysitters?" Patrick Dott begged his mother.

"Yeah, can we stay with the Jukebox Babysitters?" pleaded Jillian Clapdoodle, who was clinging onto Alana's pant leg.

"Just one more song?" Marie Willabee asked her dad.

"Pweese, Mommy?" said May Dott.

The party was better than any of us imagined. We even raised $47 in donations for the children's charity. And we each earned a pink bead!

❧ ☙

The phone rang at Katie's house six times the next morning. Six different Nickel Street parents called, and they all asked the same two questions: "When are the Jukebox Babysitters having the next party?" and "Can we sign up?"

They also said that the Jukebox Party was the last thing their kids talked about when they went to bed and the first thing they talked about when they woke up.

After the last call, Katie announced to the NSB, "It looks like the Junior Babysitters have a new name: the Jukebox Babysitters."

Junior Babysitters has the same initials as Jukebox Babysitters, I thought. *We can still use our JB T-shirts and bags.*

The last thing the NSB discussed at the Bagels-and-Babysitting Breakfast Meeting was the schedule of jobs for the coming week.

"One sec," said Katie over her shoulder as she headed down the hall to her bedroom. "I have to get my datebook so I can give everyone their babysitting assignments."

When she came back she looked upset. "That's weird," she said. "I can't find my datebook anywhere."

"When was the last time you had it?" asked Karen.

"Let me think…I believe…hmmmm…" she cupped her hand over her mouth, tilted her head and looked up into a far-off place.

"It was last Sunday morning right after I talked to Ashley-Rose," Katie said. She turned to me. "Ashley-Rose, remember you came to my house to look at the datebook? Where did you put it when you were done?"

I concentrated on a long thread hanging from the hem of my shirt and thought, *It would be just like me to be rushing again and put it in some odd place.*

I could feel six pairs of eyes looking at me. But I couldn't look back. They were waiting for my reply to a question I could not answer.

Chapter Ten

LOST & NOT FOUND

"I put it back on the bed," I blurted out. But even as I spoke I wondered, *At least I think I did.*

I helped the NSB search high and low. Under the bed. In the cupboard. Even in the freezer. Without it everyone was completely confused. Who was babysitting where? When? What time?

No one accused me of losing the datebook, but I could tell what they were all thinking. Another flub by Ashley-Rose. Zoom does it again. I hoped they would not fire the NSB Secretary for being careless*.

Hey! I'm the Secretary! I thought. How could we have forgotten that I had the entire schedule written down in my pocket-sized calendar?

"We can use my pocket calendar until we find Katie's datebook," I suggested.

Kristin smacked her forehead lightly. "That's right!"

Others exclaimed, "What a relief!" and "Thank goodness!"

My pocket-size calendar would get us through the week. But we still needed to find Katie's datebook. It had a special section for important information like the kids' birthdays and parents' emergency phone numbers.

Where could Katie's datebook have gone? I wondered. If I wanted to save my reputation* as a trustworthy future babysitter, I had to find it.

I did not find Katie's datebook that day, that week, or even that month. It had vanished. Disappeared. Poof! Gone.

The subject wasn't brought up again, but it was "there." It was "there" in the back of the NSB's minds. It was "there," clumped together with all my other "oops!" moments.

The second Jukebox Party was as fun as the first.

I don't know who had more of a ball—the kids or the Juniors. Or maybe it was the parents, who had a couple of hours to do as they pleased.

Mr. and Mrs. Dott had played tennis with Mr. and Mrs. Pizzelli. "They beat us," said Mr. Dott, "but we're challenging them to a rematch during the next Jukebox Party."

"The Jukebox Clubhouse is here to stay, right?" asked Mrs. Pizzelli.

"We could have the Jukebox Party twice a month," Katie suggested, "on the first and third Fridays of each month."

The kids cheered and the parents voted yes all around. And the Jukebox Babysitters were on cloud* nine.

77

Chapter Eleven

HURRY UP & GROW UP

"I have a great idea," I said to the NSB the next morning at the Bagels-and-Babysitting Breakfast Meeting.

Karla jumped in before I could tell my idea to the group. "Ashley-Rose, there are plenty of coins in the Nickel Jar. It would be a huge help if you rolled them."

"But about my idea—" I started, realizing that no one was paying attention.

I can't wait to hurry up and grow up and be a babysitter, I thought. *Then somebody else can roll coins.*

I went to Katie's bedroom and lifted the Nickel Jar off her desk. It weighed a ton. As I was about to leave the room, I heard the girls talking in hushed voices. That meant they were discussing something private. Something they didn't want me to hear.

Naturally I wanted to know what that something might be, so I stayed right where I was.

"What happened, Kim?" Katie said.

"Remember the night that Ashley-Rose was sick? What a disaster!" Kim said in a whisper. "She usually reads stories to the Dotts' boys while I put the girls to bed. But since she couldn't make it that night, I was on my own. Right before bedtime, Jack dropped his Happy Box."

There were lots of groans. Everyone in the NSB knows that Jack's Happy Box is a tall round tin box that contains his collection of 73 prized marbles.

Kim continued, "The marbles went rolling from one end of the room to the other. Then May slipped on one and bonked* her arm—just a little—and she started bawling.

"Jack was frustrated and started throwing marbles as fast as I could collect them. Violet needed a clean diaper, but I couldn't change it until I got May a bandage and kissed her boo-boo.

"At the same time, Patrick had snuck into the dining room and scribbled all over the wallpaper with crayons. I was still scrubbing the walls when Mr. and Mrs. Dott got home. I actually missed Ashley-Rose."

"Sometimes I think she should come with a warning label because the mistakes she makes are doozies*," said Karen, "but she can also be very helpful."

"Definitely," said Katie. "She does the small but important

79

stuff, like fetching diapers and finding the toothpaste cap that the kids always forget to put back on the tube."

"What about that clean-up trick she does," added Karla, "where she pretends the kids are on a scavenger hunt to find all their toys. The toys are back on the shelves and in the bins in about two minutes!"

I would have liked to hear more about how wonderful I am, but Katie called my name. "Ashley-Rose, did you find the Nickel Jar?"

Skipping down the hallway, I heard a sharp "Shhh! Here she comes. We don't want to give her any more 'ideas'!"

❧ ☙

I had never in my whole life been as scared as I was a couple of weeks later when I was helping Katie babysit 11-month-old Dennis Pizzelli.

Dennis was a little cranky when his parents left the house at 6:15 p.m. Even after a warm bottle and a burp, he was still not his usual smiling self.

Katie put him into his crib and let me turn on the baby monitors. One stays on his nightstand. I tucked the other one into my pocket so we could hear Dennis if he woke up.

Not long after, while we were playing our second game of cards, Dennis started whimpering. Then he let out a long, loud cry. Jumping out of our chairs, we sprinted to his bedroom.

Katie picked him up and knew immediately that he had a fever. I felt his forehead and he was hot to the touch.

I panicked. *What should we do?* I didn't know the answer but Katie did.

She asked me to get the baby thermometer. *Walk, do not run*, I thought to myself. *You don't want to trip and break*

the thermometer. She took Dennis's temperature and it was 102 degrees.

Next, Katie asked me to get her phone out of her babysitting bag. She rocked the baby and told me Mr. Pizzelli's phone number. I pressed each button carefully so I wouldn't make a mistake and have to start over.

Mr. Pizzelli answered his phone on the second ring and told Katie that they would be home ASAP*. Katie suggested that we call my mom since she is a nurse, to let her know what was going on. She said she'd come right over if we needed her.

As we waited for the Pizzellis to get home, Katie calmly reassured me that the baby was going to be fine.

Thank goodness Katie's here, I thought.

When we heard Dennis's parents finally pull their car into the driveway, we both breathed sighs of relief.

On the walk home, Katie put her arm around my shoulder. "Good job tonight, Ashley-Rose," she said. I noticed that she did not call me Zoom.

Chapter Twelve

ZANY WORKS

What do you do with siblings who constantly squabble*? Or a baby who won't stop crying? Or a little girl who misses her mommy? Or picky eaters determined to pitch their half-chewed raisins, drippy watermelon or sticky bananas around the room from their highchairs?

That's easy. Chug around the room like a choo-choo train. Make mud pies. Act like a mummy. Waddle like a duck and "quack-quack." Do a magic trick. Let the pink bunny hand puppet tell a story about a ladybug that takes a magic carpet ride on a leaf around the world. Plug your nose, sing a song and pretend you're swimming underwater.

Being zany works. Kids love zany. Silliness distracts them from whatever is bugging them. If they're tired, bored, annoyed, hot or fidgety*, the more nonsense* you can dish up the better. Which is fine with me.

Let the NSB handle the stinky diapers and high fevers and staying awake until midnight when the parents come home.

For the time being, I'd rather be getting a game of kickball going in the Dotts' backyard, playing Eye Spy Something Round/Square/Big/Small/Red/Blue with Marie Willabee or letting Stanley Swanson beat me in Go Fish.

I'm pretty lucky I get to do all the fun stuff. As a matter of fact, I'm just plain lucky.

Top 10 Reasons I'm Lucky

#1: The Jukebox Babysitters Rock! That's not bragging, it's what our new T-shirts say (thanks to the NSB).
#2: Our Friday night Jukebox Parties raised $182 in donations! The NSB and Jukebox Babysitters went on a shopping trip together and we bought backpacks.

Then we filled them with pencils, markers, notebooks and erasers, plus granola bars for snacks. Now four kids will have the supplies they need to do their schoolwork.
#3: I found a sound that makes me as happy as

Slowpoke purring. It's Marybeth and Jillian laughing like crazy when I pretend I'm a crab scuttling* along on their bedroom floor. This leads me to #4.

#4: Scuttling on their bedroom floor is how I found Katie's datebook. Remember how the Clapdoodles were having lunch at Aunt Barb's the day it disappeared?

After I put the datebook back on Katie's bed, Jillian went "pretend shopping" in the bedroom, tucked the datebook in her princess bag and later put it in her special hiding place under her bed.

#5: The NSB came up with a way for the Jukebox Babysitters to get more babysitting experience. When a parent is going to be home, but needs help with the kids while they are making dinner or doing laundry, a Jukebox Babysitter can go over to play with them.

#6: At the last NSB meeting, I found a big box wrapped in lime-green paper with a bright pink bow on my babysitter club chair. The tag read: "To the Official NSB Secretary and Coin Roller."

Imagine my joy when I tore open the paper and found a battery-operated coin sorter inside. Now all I'll have to do is dump the coins into the machine and it will sort and count pennies, nickels, dimes and quarters. It even stacks them into the brown paper wrappers.

#7: A few of Katie's friends from school who live across town came to an NSB meeting. They want to learn how they can set up a babysitting club like the NSB in their own neighborhood. And guess what? They interviewed me because they want to have a Secretary, too!

#8: I earned two new beads for my Babysitting Bracelet!

#9: It takes a long time to grow up, but it's actually been a really fun long time.

#10: I have a great idea! A Jukebox Clubhouse Summer Camp. I can't wait to suggest it at the next NSB meeting. ☺

Glossary

*Many words have more than one meaning. Here are the definitions of words marked with this symbol ** (an asterisk) as they are used in sentences.*

ASAP: *As Soon As Possible*
blare: *loud sound*
bonked: *hit*
bungle: *to goof up*
buzz: *sounds of excitement*
careless: *not giving a task enough attention*
chorused: *said at the same time*
chuckled: *laughed quietly*
cloud, as in "on cloud nine": *extremely happy*
cymbals: *round metal plates with handles that make a ringing sound when struck together*
dim: *dark*
doozies: *things that stand out*
drenched: *soaked, wet*
fidgety: *making movements because of being nervous or impatient*

flub: *mistake*

flurry: *a large amount*

hassle: *an annoying problem*

hastily: *quickly*

heated: *starting to get angry*

hind: *back*

hollow: *having an empty space on the inside*

key: *important*

logo: *a special symbol* used to identify a group*

miniature: *a very small copy of something that is usually bigger*

muttered: *spoke in a low voice or grumbled*

noggin: *a person's head*

nonsense: *foolish or silly behavior*

promote: *to give someone a better job*

rafters: *long pieces of wood that are used to hold up a pointed roof*

reputation: *what people think about a person*

rummaged: *searched through by moving things around*

RSVP: *let someone who is giving a party know if you will or will not be able to go*

scowled: *looked irritated*

scuttling: *moving quickly, scurrying*

smirk: *smile in a silly way*

spruced, as in "spruced up": *fixed up, neatened up*

squabble: *argue noisily*

stuffy: *having no fresh air*

stung: *hurt*

symbol: *a sign that stands for a certain thing*

trove: *a group of delightful things*

tune, as in "changed her tune": *behaved in a different way*

umpteenth: *a large number*

Rainy day? Put on a Puppet Play!

There's a good reason why puppets have been popular for 4000 years—they're as fun to make as they are to play with. Entertain young kids like Ashley-Rose did in the story, or put on a puppet play at your next family get-together.

Create your own puppets with odds and ends found around your house. Possibilities are everywhere you look. Start with felt (like the one below), or use a sock, a wooden spoon or an empty cardboard paper towel tube. With a little imagination and white glue, popcorn or pasta spirals can be turned into a funny head of hair, bottle caps become eyes, yarn makes whiskers and pipe cleaners form eyeglasses.

91

Ashley-Rose's No-Sew Bunny Puppet

1. It's easy to make this sweet bunny. All you'll need is white glue, scissors, two sheets of pink felt, one sheet of white felt, buttons and pink and blue fine-point felt-tipped markers.

2. If an adult can help you use a copy machine, make an enlargement of the bunny outline (see the next page) so it's about one inch wider than your hand on both sides and the top. Then cut around the enlarged outline, trace the bunny shape onto both pieces of pink felt and cut the shapes out. If you're not using a copy machine, you can draw the bunny outline onto a piece of pink felt, making it about one inch wider than your hand on both sides and the top. Cut the shape out. Trace that shape onto a second piece of felt and cut it out.

3. On one of the felt bunny shapes, put a thick outline of white glue all around the edges, but not on the bottom. Place the second piece on top of the first and gently press the edges together. Glue on buttons for eyes (we put one button on top of another for one of the eyes), and pieces of white felt for the ears, tummy and teeth. Let it dry overnight.

4. Once the glue has dried, use markers to draw a pink heart-shaped nose and smile. Outline the tummy and ears in pink, then add tiny lines to give it the look of "stitches." Outline one tooth in blue and one in green. Draw blue hearts on the paws.

5. Slip your hand inside, give your puppet personality, and charm a crowd!

Remember, craft projects should always
be supervised by your parent or a trusted adult.
Small items should be kept away from smaller children at all times.

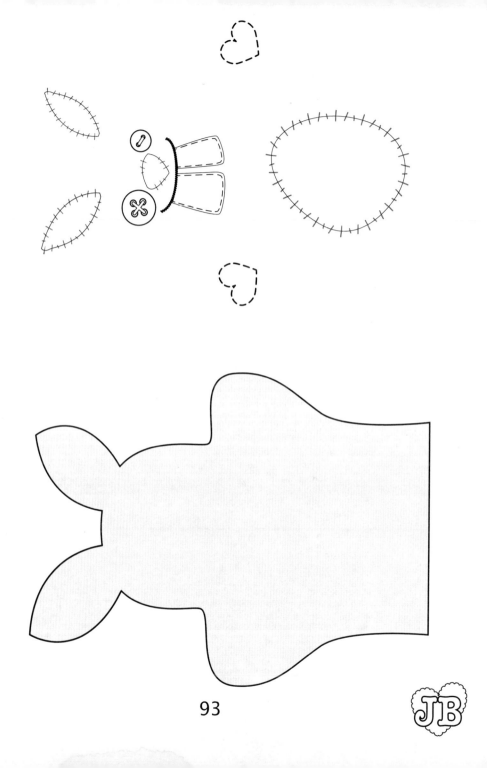

93

About the Author

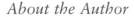

Susan Cappadonia Love lives in Milton, Massachusetts with her husband, Scott, and daughters, Sophie and Olivia.

*In addition to **The Jukebox Babysitters**, she has also written five other books in the Our Generation® Series, **The Dress in the Window, The Sweet Shoppe Mystery, The Mystery of the Vanishing Coin, Stars in Your Eyes** and **One Smart Cookie**, as well as other children's books.*

Much gratitude goes to all the wonderful people at Battat Incorporated, including Mylene Vallee, Julie Kassabian, Batia Tarrab, Alison Morin, Joe Battat, Dany Battat and Natalie Cohen. Many thanks to my friends and colleagues, Gisela Voss, Kate Annantuonio, Pam Shrimpton and Julie Driscoll.